THAT'S GOOD! THAT'S BAD!

IN THE GRAND CANYON

MARGERY CUYLER

ILLUSTRATED BY
DAVID CATROW

Henry Holt and Company
New York

Henry Holt and Company, LLC
Publishers since 1866
175 Fifth Avenue
New York, New York 10010
www.HenryHoltKids.com

Library of Congress Cataloging-in-Publication Data
Cuyler, Margery.
That's good! That's bad! in the Grand Canyon / Margery Cuyler; pictures by David Catrow.
Summary: When a little boy vacations at the Grand Canyon with his grandmother,
both good and bad things happen.
[1. Grandmothers—Fiction. 2. Grand Canyon (Ariz.)—Fiction.
3. Tall tales.] I. Catrow, David, ill. II. Title.
PZ7.C997 Th 2001 [E]—dc21   00-057534

ISBN-13: 978-0-8050-5975-5 / ISBN-10: 0-8050-5975-X
First Edition—2002 / Book design by David Caplan
Printed in China on acid-free paper. ∞

3 5 7 9 10 8 6 4

The artist used pen and ink and watercolor on
watercolor paper to create the illustrations for this book.

For Jul and Joe, in memory of some wonderful hikes
—M. C.

To Hillary and D.J.—I love you dearly (II)
—D. C.

One day a little boy and his grandmother rode to the Grand Canyon for their summer vacation.

Oh, that's good.
No, that's BAD!

As they hiked down Bright Angel Trail, the little boy was careless, OH, DEAR! He slipped and fell over the edge of the path, OOPS!

Oh, that's bad.
No, that's GOOD!

He dropped to the back of a mule,
GIDDYAP!, that was walking down
the switchbacks to the bottom of
the canyon, WHAT LUCK!

Oh, that's good.
No, that's BAD!

The mule was so startled that he sped
down the trail as fast as he could go,
CLIPPITY-CLOP. The little boy held on
tight. He jounced and bounced until
his teeth rattled and his knees shook,
CLACKETY-CLACK!

Oh, that's bad.
No, that's GOOD!

The mule raced with the little boy to the Colorado River, TROT, TROT. When it reached the edge, it stopped suddenly. The little boy was thrown over its head into a raft being paddled by a group of friendly tourists, SWISH, SWISH!

Oh, that's good.
No, *that's **BAD!***

The raft drifted into some choppy rapids. The little boy yelled and hollered, HELP, as the boat hit a big rock, BUMP! The little boy flew over the side into the foamy water, SPLASH!

Oh, that's bad.
No, that's GOOD!

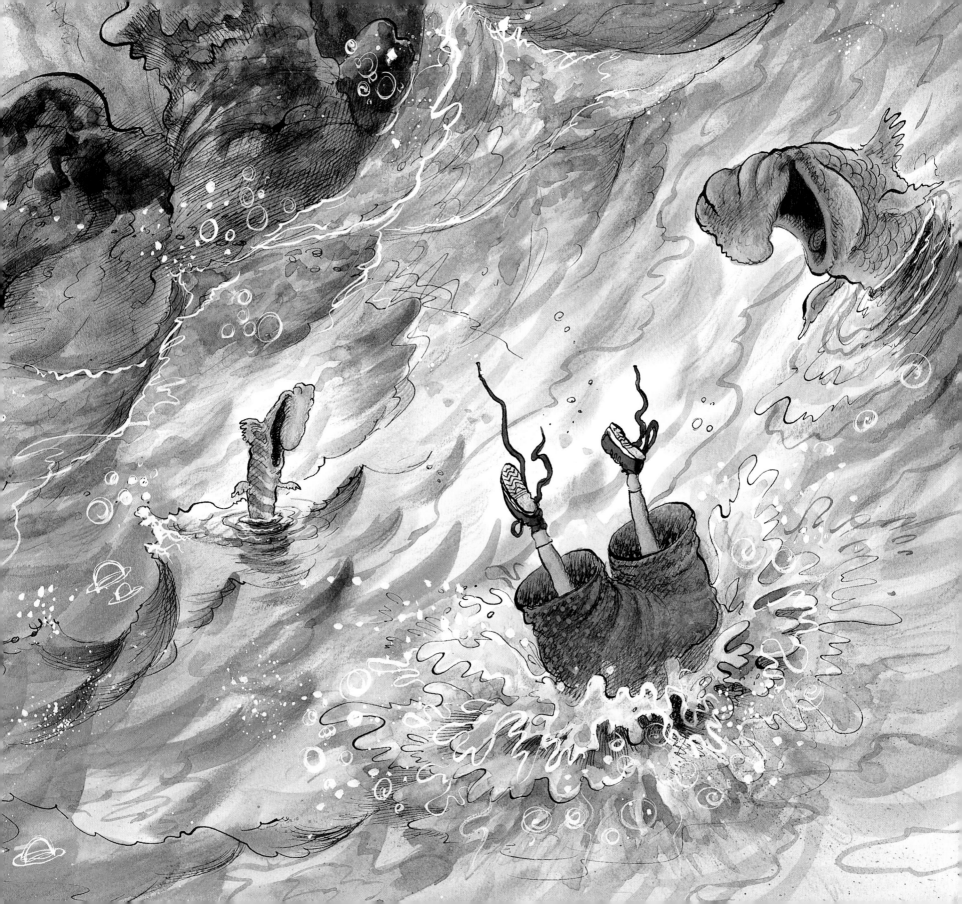

The current swept the little boy along and tossed
him onto a sandy beach. A helicopter was rescuing
some visitors whose boat had capsized, OOPSY-DAISY!
The little boy's backpack got caught on a runner, and
he was lifted up, up, and away, WHOOSH!

Oh, that's good.
No, that's BAD!

As the helicopter picked up speed,
the little boy's pack slipped free,
UH-OH! He fell toward a rocky cliff
in the valley below, EEEE-eee!

Oh, that's bad.
No, that's GOOD!

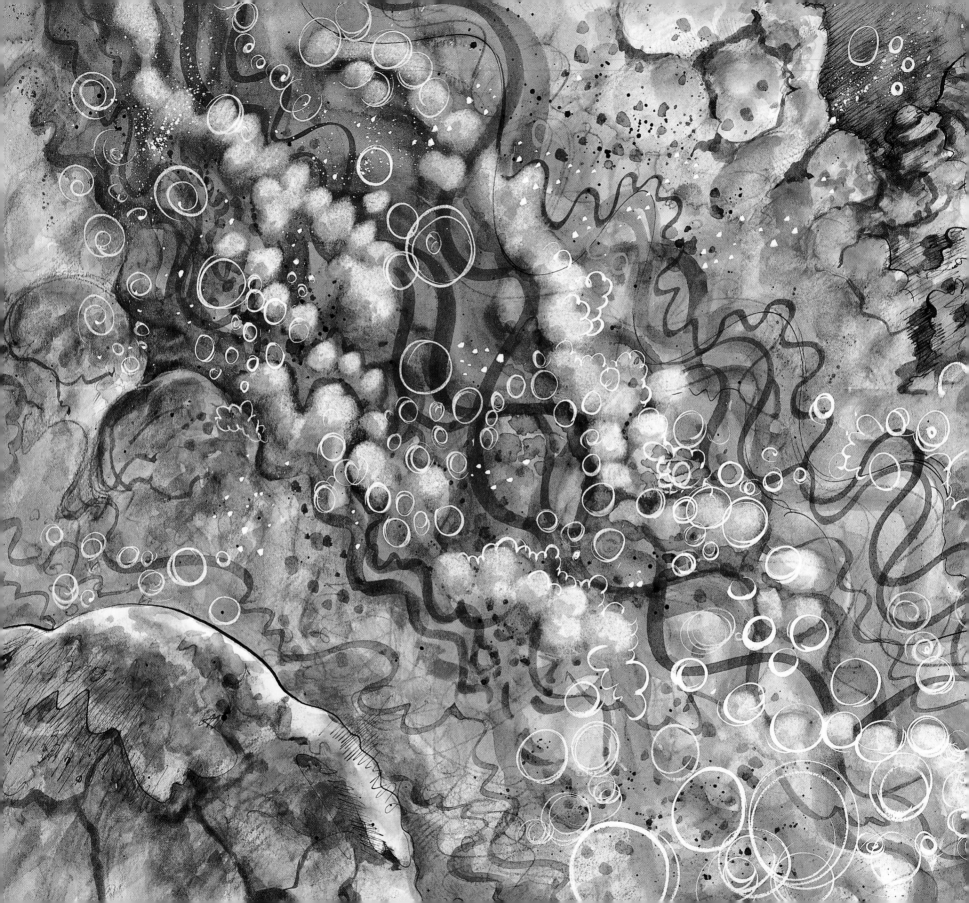

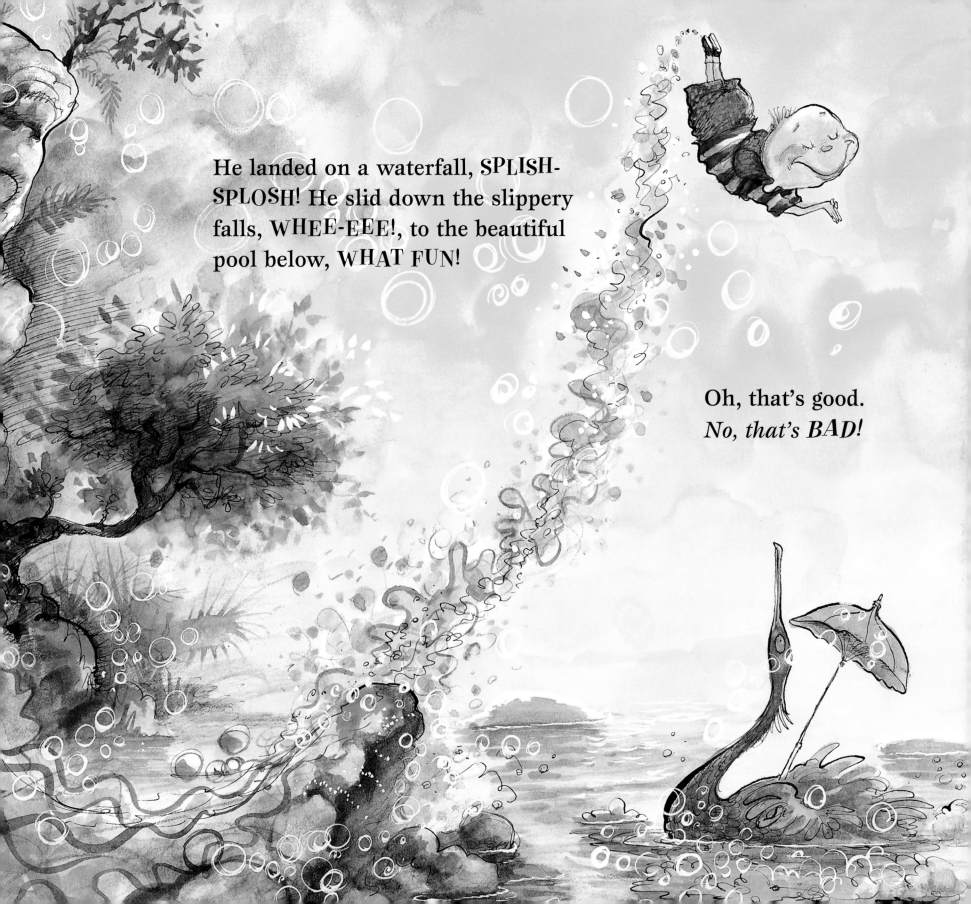

He landed on a waterfall, SPLISH-SPLOSH! He slid down the slippery falls, WHEE-EEE!, to the beautiful pool below, WHAT FUN!

Oh, that's good.
No, that's BAD!

The water churned and whirled at the bottom of the falls, BISH-BASH! The little boy was thrown under the surface. He spun around as if he were inside a washing machine, CHURLA, CHURLA!

Oh, that's bad.
No, that's GOOD!

A Havasupai Indian fished the little boy out of the water,
THANK GOODNESS! He set the little boy on the back of a
horse and led him on the trail to Supai Village, CLIP-CLOP!

Oh, that's good.
No, that's BAD!

The horse stepped on a rattlesnake that was sunning itself on a rock by the path, RATTA-RATTA! The horse galloped up the path to the village, JUGGA-JUGGA!

Oh, that's bad.
No, that's GOOD!

The little boy's grandmother was waiting for him at the top of the trail, HOORAY! The Havasupai had radioed ahead that the little boy was all right, PHEW! The grandmother was so happy to see him, she gave him a big hug, OOMPH!, and then another one, WOW!

Oh, that's GOOD!

*Yes, that **IS** good!*

She set the little boy on her shoulders, and that's where he stayed for the rest of the vacation!